Scratch and Sniff

by Margaret Ryan
illustrated by Nathan Reed

PICTURE WINDOW BOOKS
Minneapolis, Minnesota

Editor: Nick Healy
Page Production: Brandie Shoemaker
Art Director: Nathan Gassman
Associate Managing Editor: Christianne Jones

First American edition published in 2007 by
Picture Window Books
5115 Excelsior Boulevard
Suite 232
Minneapolis, MN 55416
877-845-8392
www.picturewindowbooks.com

First published in 2006 by A&C Black Publishers Limited, 38 Soho Square,
London W1D 3HB, with the title SCRATCH AND SNIFF.

Text copyright © 2006 Margaret Ryan
Illustrations copyright © 2006 Nathan Reed

Printed in the United States of America.

Library of Congress Cataloging-in-Publication Data
Ryan, Margaret, 1944-
Scratch and Sniff / by Margaret Ryan ; illustrated by Nathan Reed.
p. cm. — (Read-it! chapter books)
Summary: When the local furniture store is robbed, Scratch and Sniff, the
local doggy "Secret Service," help their master, Police Officer Penny
Penrose, solve the crime.
ISBN-13: 978-1-4048-3130-8 (library binding)
ISBN-10: 1-4048-3130-4 (library binding)
[1. Dogs—Fiction. 2. Robbers and outlaws—Fiction. 3. Mystery and
detective stories.] I. Reed, Nathan, ill. II. Title.
PZ7.R9543Sc 2006
[Fic]—dc22   2006027265

Table of Contents

Chapter One

Scratch and Sniff were curled up in a corner in the kitchen, trying to take a nap. But it wasn't easy. Police officer Penny Penrose was late for work again.

"Has anyone seen my bicycle lock?" she asked.

Scratch scratched, then wandered over to the kitchen door and barked.

"Well done, Scratch," said Penny. She removed the bicycle lock from the door handle. Then she looked around again.

"Has anyone seen my bicycle helmet?" Penny asked.

Sniff sniffed, then waddled underneath the kitchen table, wagged his tail, and barked.

"Well done, Sniff," said Penny. She picked up the helmet and put it on. "Now, you boys eat up your breakfast, and I'll see you later."

Penny hurried outside, jumped on her old bike, and pedaled off to the police station.

Scratch yawned and scratched.
Sniff yawned and sniffed.

"Should we stroll over and check
out the food, Sniff?" asked Scratch.

"Good idea, Scratch," said Sniff.

What they found wasn't so good.

"Yuck!" said Scratch. "Nothing
but dry chunks again."

"What does Penny think we are?" asked Sniff. "House cats?"

Scratch shook his shaggy collie head. Sniff wiggled his sleek dachshund body.

It was time for some decent food, they agreed, and they headed out through the doggy door. They stopped at Mrs. Pudding's bakery.

Mrs. Pudding was piling up trays filled with fresh cupcakes, doughnuts, and jelly rolls when the dogs arrived.

"Good morning, boys," she smiled. "Would you like your usual?"

Scratch and Sniff barked and wagged their tails, and then the two of them settled down outside the shop to enjoy their jelly rolls. They had just gotten to the mushy part in the middle when they heard a siren.

Lights flashed, tires screeched, and Sergeant Snide roared past in his police car.

"Looks like Snide is on a case," said Scratch.

"One he will probably bungle again," said Sniff. "Let's go and see Penny."

The dogs bounded along the road to the police station.

Penny was standing outside, surrounded by traffic cones.

"I thought you boys might show up," she said. "Chief Hector just told me there has been a robbery at Doogood's Furniture Store. As usual, Sergeant Snide has gone off to investigate by himself. He left me here to count traffic cones."

Penny sighed and exclaimed, "It's not fair!"

Scratch and Sniff looked at each other. Perhaps they could help Penny solve the crime.

"Looks like a case for the doggy secret service," said Scratch.

"Let's take the shortcut to Doogood's Furniture Store and do some checking around ourselves," said Sniff.

Chapter Two

The dogs headed off down side streets and alleyways. They dodged dirty garbage cans, leapt over litter, and outran cranky cats.

Finally, they stopped near Doogood's Furniture Store. They watched from the sidewalk across the street.

They were just
in time to see
Sergeant Snide
march up to the
entrance of the
shop, where the
store manager
was waiting.

"I am
Sergeant Snide,"
he bellowed,
"and I
can spot a
crook a mile
away. Take me to the crime scene
immediately."

"Certainly," said the manager.
"Come this way."

Scratch and Sniff looked at each other.

"While the great detective is busy inside, should we look around outside?" asked Scratch.

"Good idea," said Sniff. "We might be able to sniff out a few clues on our own."

"We cannot be seen, though," said Scratch. "I'll have to slither along on my belly."

"Mine nearly touches the ground anyway," said Sniff.

The dogs sneaked past the shop window and slipped around the corner to the back of the store. A large van was parked there. It had "Doogood's Furniture" written on the side.

Suddenly, a door opened, and two men in brown uniforms came out carrying a sofa. They puffed and panted as they heaved the sofa into the back of the van.

"That's strange," whispered Scratch. "Those men must work at Doogood's. But Sergeant Snide shouldn't be letting anyone go. He should be keeping them all inside for questioning."

"Snide's brains are in his boots," muttered Sniff. "Let's get a closer look at these guys."

The dogs edged toward the van. They were just in time to hear the taller of the two men hiss, "Are you sure you stashed the money away safely, Bernie?"

"Stuffed it in the middle cushion, Stan," Bernie replied.

"That sergeant was a real fool," Stan said with a laugh.

The men climbed into the cab and started the engine.

"They're the robbers!" gasped Scratch. "And they're getting away with the money!"

"We have to do something," said Sniff, "and fast."

Scratch and Sniff looked at each other.

"Cones!" they both barked.

Chapter Three

Scratch and Sniff headed back up
side streets and alleyways. They
outran cranky cats, leapt over litter,
and dodged dirty garbage cans until
they arrived at the police station.

"Good," said Scratch. "The cones are still here. All we have to do is push one pile down the street to the intersection."

"And block off the other road," added Sniff. "That way the Doogood's van will have to come down High Street, right past the police station. But we'd better be quick. There's no time to lose."

The dogs hurried over to the nearest pile of cones.

"This will be easy," said Scratch. "When I was a champion sheepdog, I was great at nudging sheep in the right direction."

"Then you can show me what to do," said Sniff. "I've only ever been a champion nap-taker."

Scratch nudged and pushed.

Sniff pushed and nudged.

Eventually the pile of cones reached the intersection. Then Sniff held up a paw to stop the traffic, while Scratch toppled over the cones and lined them up across the road.

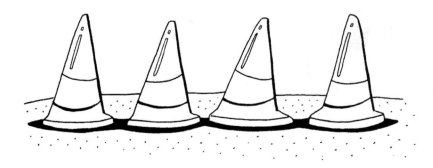

"Just look at those amazing dogs," said passers-by. "What next?"

Scratch and Sniff hurried back to the police station. Penny was standing outside, and she looked very puzzled.

"There you are, boys," she said. "I was wondering where you'd gone. Have you seen a pile of cones? I seem to have lost them."

Then she saw that all of the cars
on High Street had come to a halt.

"What's causing the traffic jam?"
she wondered aloud.

She was on her way to find out
when she noticed the Doogood's van.

"What's that doing here? Sergeant
Snide shouldn't be allowing any vans
to leave," she said.

Scratch and Sniff looked at each other happily.

"Well done, Penny!" they both barked. "Good thinking!"

Chapter Four

Penny, followed by Scratch and Sniff, headed through the traffic jam to the Doogood's van.

The police officer rapped on
the window and said, "Can I have a
word with you?"

Bernie glanced at Stan, then rolled
down the window.

"Certainly, officer, how can I help
you?" he asked.

"What are you carrying in your
van?" asked Penny.

"Furniture," said Bernie. "See, it says so on the side of the van—Doogood's Furniture."

"That's the clue," giggled Stan.

"Would you open the back of your van, please?" asked Penny. "I'd like to take a look."

"If you must, officer," sighed Bernie. "But it's just furniture, and we're late for the delivery as it is."

Bernie and Stan got out and unlocked the back of the van.

"There you are," said Bernie. "One three-cushion sofa to be delivered to Mrs. Patterson on Barnton Street."

Penny looked in the van. It was completely empty, other than the sofa. She climbed inside and walked all around the sofa, then peered underneath it.

"There certainly doesn't seem to be anything out of place," she said.

"Then we'll be on our way, officer," said Bernie.

"As soon as you clear up this traffic jam," added Stan.

Penny started to get out of the van, so Scratch and Sniff had to act quickly.

"We need to let Penny know what is hidden in that middle cushion, or the robbers will get away!" barked Scratch.

Sniff nodded.

"That sofa looks very comfortable," he said. "Feel like taking a nap?"

Chapter Five

Scratch jumped up onto the sofa. Sniff jumped, too. He got his front paws onto the sofa. He struggled to climb onto the top.

"The rest of me will be along shortly, Scratch," he said, panting as his back end scrambled up.

"What are you doing?" asked Penny. "Get down this minute!"

"Yeah, clear off, you lousy mutts," muttered Bernie.

Scratch and Sniff ignored him and lay down.

"Scratch! Sniff! You'll ruin the sofa with your dirty paws!" said Penny.

"Dirty paws?" said Scratch. "Then we'd better clean them. Don't you agree, Sniff?"

Scratch began to scratch away at
the middle cushion.
Scratch! Scratch!

"Can't have dirty paws," agreed
Sniff, and he joined in.
Scratch! Scratch!

Then they pushed the middle cushion onto the floor and scratched at it again.

Scratch! Scratch!

"Control those dogs, or we'll have to file a complaint, officer!" yelled Bernie and Stan.

"Be quiet!" said Penny. "I think the dogs are trying to tell me something. What is it?"

Scratch and Sniff looked at each other happily again.

"She's got it at last!" they barked.

Officer Penrose picked up the cushion and opened the zipper. Bundles of money fell out.

"Run for it, Stan!" cried Bernie. "The jig is up!"

But Stan was already out of the van and running down the middle of High Street.

Bernie followed close behind.

"They're getting away!" cried Penny. "After them!"

Scratch bounded after Stan and pulled him down. THUD! SMACK!

Sniff bounded after Bernie and tripped him. THUD! SMACK!

Penny caught up with them all. She grabbed Bernie and Stan.

"You're through," she said with a grin. Then she marched them back to the police station.

Sergeant Snide arrived just as
Penny was counting the piles of
stolen money.

"What's that?" he demanded.

"The money from Doogood's
Furniture Store," said Penny.
"Scratch and Sniff helped me catch
the robbers."

"I'm taking Officer Penrose and the dogs to Mrs. Pudding's bakery to celebrate," said Chief Hector.

Sergeant Snide frowned and stomped off.

"Congratulations, Officer Penrose. You solved the case," Chief Hector said with a smile.

"Thank you," said Penny, blushing. "But the credit should really go to Scratch and Sniff."

In the bakery, the dogs barked and wagged their tails. They liked solving problems. Now they had another one—which delicious treat should they choose?

"I feel like a jelly roll," said Scratch.

"That's funny," said Sniff. "You look like a collie!"

Look for More *Read-it!* Chapter Books

The Badcat Gang
Beastly Basil
Cat Baby
Cleaner Genie
Clever Monkeys
Contest Crazy
Disgusting Denzil
Duperball
Elvis the Squirrel
Eric's Talking Ears
High Five Hank
Hot Dog and the Talent Competition
Nelly the Monstersitter
On the Ghost Trail
Sid and Bolter
Stan the Dog Becomes Superdog
The Thing in the Basement

Looking for a specific title? A complete list
of *Read-it!* Chapter Books is available on our Web site:
www.picturewindowbooks.com